This vacation Bible school inspired the Bible Buddy named Zion. Zion is a lion, and lions are one of God's most powerful creatures. Zion reminds kids that, even when life is sad,

God is good!

Best of Buddies
Boohoo to Woohoo! God Is Always Good
Written by **JEFF WHITE**   *Illustrated by* **LUIS GADEA**

Group | lifetree™

MyLifetree.com
Loveland, CO

Copyright © 2019 Group Publishing, Inc./0000 0001 0362 4853
Lifetree™ is an imprint of Group Publishing, Inc. Visit our website: **group.com**

Author: Jeff White
Illustrator: Luis Gadea
Chief Creative Officer: Joani Schultz
Senior Editor: Candace McMahan
Designer: RoseAnne Sather
Assistant Editor: Cherie Shifflett

Scripture quotations are taken from the Holy Bible, New Living Translation, copyright © 1996, 2004, 2015 by Tyndale House Foundation. Used by permission of Tyndale House Publishers, Inc., Carol Stream, Illinois 60188. All rights reserved.

Library of Congress Cataloging-in-Publication Data
Names: White, Jeff, 1968- author. | Gadea, Luis, illustrator.
Title: Boohoo to woohoo! : God is always good / written by Jeff White ;
  illustrated by Luis Gadea.
Description: Loveland, CO : Group Publishing, Inc., [2019] | Series: Best of
  buddies | Summary: "Zion the lion, a character from Group's Roar VBS
  program, shows three of his distraught friends how God can turn sad
  events into happy ones"-- Provided by publisher.
Identifiers: LCCN 2018041409 (print) | LCCN 2018048381 (ebook) | ISBN
  9781470757199 (ePub) | ISBN 9781470757243 (first American hardcover)
Classification: LCC PZ7.1.W443 (ebook) | LCC PZ7.1.W443 Bo 2019 (print) | DDC
  [E]--dc23
LC record available at https://lccn.loc.gov/2018041409

978-1-4707-5724-3 (hardcover)
978-1-4707-5719-9 (ePub)
Printed in China.
001 China 1218

10 9 8 7 6 5 4 3 2 1   28 27 26 25 24 23 22 21 20 19

Zion the lion woke up in the grass.
He blinked his eyes open, glad to see the sun
shining after a blustery storm the night before.

All of a sudden he heard
the saddest sound he'd ever heard.

"Oh no, oh no, oh no!" wailed a voice.

Zion turned and saw Hooper the hoopoe bird starting to cry.
"Hooper!" the lion said. "What's wrong, little one?"

"It's my tree!" said Hooper,
"The blustery storm knocked it over.
It can't be fixed!
Now I don't have anywhere to sleep!"

"That is very sad," said Zion, shaking his head.
"Very sad, indeed. But if there's one thing I know for sure,
it's that God cares about you.
You see, when life is sad—"

But Zion was cut off
by another sad sound.

"Oh dear, oh dear, oh dear!" cried the voice.

The lion leaped away to find
Jambo the meerkat bawling like a baby.

"Jambo!" Zion said. "What's wrong, little one?"

"It's my blanket!" said Jambo.
"That blustery storm blew it into the bushes,
   and now it's in tatters.
   It can't be fixed! I'll never be comfy again!"

"How awful!" said the lion,
   wiping the tears from Jambo's cheeks.
"But remember that God cares about you.
   God can take your sad things and—"

   Again, Zion was stopped short
   by the sound of sobbing.

"Oh my, oh my, oh my!" howled the voice.

The lion sprang off toward Babette the
baboon, whose tears fell like a waterfall.

"Babette!" said Zion.
"What's wrong, little one?"

"It's my parasol!" said Babette.
"The blustery storm twisted it in all the wrong directions.
It can't be fixed! My shade is gone forever!"

"There, there," said the lion, patting the baboon on the shoulder.
"What a sad, sad day. I've seen more tears than last night's rain!"

"But hear me out," Zion said.
"God sees your tears.
God hears your cries.
God feels your sadness.
God is good, my friends.
God is *very* good!"

The three little friends
looked at Zion and said,
"We know God is good. But we're still sad.
Can God fix what's broken?"

"God can do way better
than fix your broken things.
When God turns sad things
into good things, you might
be in for a big surprise,"
said the lion.

"Follow me."

Zion led them to Hooper's broken tree.
He wove together the broken branches and
cleared a cozy spot beneath the fallen trunk.

"Hooper's tree isn't fit for a bird anymore," the lion said,
"but its shade can protect Babette from the sun.
It's even better than a parasol!"

"Woohoo!" shouted Babette.

Next, Zion took
the meerkat's shredded blanket,
reached up into a tall tree,
and shaped it into a super-soft nest.

"Jambo's blanket isn't much of a blanket anymore,"
the lion said, "but it's more than good enough
for a new nest for Hooper.
You couldn't ask for a better bed!"

"Woohoo!" squawked Hooper.

Finally, Zion took hold of the baboon's broken parasol. He took out its spokes and splinters, then wrapped its beautiful cloth around the meerkat's shoulders.

"Babette's parasol isn't good for shade anymore," the lion said, "but it makes the finest blanket I've ever seen. It fits Jambo like a glove!"

"Woohoo!" squeaked Jambo.

Hooper nestled down in his new nest.

Jambo bundled up in his beautiful blanket.

And Babette settled into her soothing shade.

"God heard your **boohoos**.
He knows when you're sad,"
said Zion the lion with a smile.
"And God heard your **woohoos**, too!
He loves to bring you joy!"

"The Lord is close to the
brokenhearted; he rescues those
whose spirits are crushed."

(Psalm 34:18)